BUNKHOUSE JOURNAL

BUNKHOUSE JOURNAL

DIANE JOHNSTON HAMM

CHARLES SCRIBNER'S SONS | NEW YORK

Collier Macmillan Canada · Toronto
Maxwell Macmillan International Publishing Group
New York · Oxford · Singapore · Sydney

The author acknowledges a debt of gratitude to the late Elinore Pruitt Stewart, whose 1913 book, *Letters of a Woman Homesteader*, revealed an inspiring love and respect for the people and land of southwestern Wyoming.

Copyright © 1990 by Diane Johnston Hamm

Charles Scribner's Sons Books for Young Readers
Macmillan Publishing Company
866 Third Avenue, New York, New York 10022

Collier Macmillan Canada, Inc.
1200 Eglinton Avenue East, Suite 200
Don Mills, Ontario M3C 3N1

First Edition   10 9 8 7 6 5 4 3 2 1
Printed in the United States of America

Library of Congress Cataloging-in-Publication Data
Hamm, Diane Johnston.
Bunkhouse journal/Diane Johnston Hamm.—1st ed.   p.   cm.
Summary: Sandy, a sensitive sixteen-year-old boy spending the winter of 1911 helping his cousins on their ranch in Wyoming, records in his journal his first love and his attempts to sort through his confused feelings for his drunkard father in Denver.
[1. Ranch life—Fiction.   2. Fathers and sons—Fiction.
3. Diaries—Fiction.]   I. Title.
PZ7.H1837Bu   1990   [Fic]—dc20   90-8062   CIP   AC
ISBN 0-684-19206-3

For Ed and Jeff, for Dad and my brothers,
and in memory of Howard and Bror

SEPTEMBER 8, 1910

Winter's coming on. I'll be staying—here at John and my cousin Karen's sheep ranch where I have worked the summer.

John is put out. He expected I would leave with the other hands after getting the sheep to the railroad in Rock Springs. I overheard him say to Karen he didn't intend to "feed that kid to sit on his butt all winter." As though I didn't expect to earn my keep!

He told me he'd try to find me a place on another ranch, that he only keeps Ed, his regular hand, on over winter.

Ed told him at dinnertime, though, that I needed a home here worse than he did. He said he was all saddled up. He'd be back in spring to help with the plowing.

John was plenty mad. It didn't matter that Ed said he'd choose me over other greenhorns he's worked alongside. John made it clear I'm no substitute.

Without Ed and the others here, the emptiness in

the bunkhouse bears down on a person like a wind through the canyon.

SEPTEMBER 9, 1910

John's still sore about my being here. And he's mad, too, about the price he got for his sheep in Rock Springs.

Karen tried to cheer him up at supper by opening a can of store-bought peaches. She'd made a plate of shortbread, which she said is one of the few things to come out right every time since it only takes three ingredients and doesn't have to rise.

When she passed John's chair, she touched his shoulder and thanked him for bringing her back peppermints from Rock Springs.

All he said was, "Humpf!" as though no peaches, thanks, or shortbread could make him feel better. Then he lowered his head into his hands and added, "I'm so glad to be rid of those damn sheep. I could go out and shoot what's left of them right now."

I excused myself from the table, figuring he needed to be alone with Karen.

SEPTEMBER 10, 1910

John said today he never pays Ed wages over winter—just feeds him for a few hours' work each day and help with the early lambing. He said he'd offer me no more and expect no less.

I helped him haul two barrels of empty cans to a dump in the hills behind the bunkhouse. A dead cow, a neighbor's, died of bloat up there. Did it ever stink.

Karen gave me an armload of bedclothes she gets out for Ed each winter—a flour-sack quilt stuffed with feathers, a Hudson's Bay blanket, and an antelope-skin rug to put by the bed. She said the bunkhouse will be tolerably warm if I close the door between the two rooms.

She gave me a dented teakettle to warm water in on the potbelly stove everyone calls the "Captain." There's a tin cup with Ed's name on it, a box of tea leaves, and a hinged strainer spoon for steeping the leaves.

I asked Karen if Ed would have trouble finding a job. She said not to worry about him. Many places can use a man who's good at woodworking like he is. (Ed's the one who carved the horse heads on the wall above each bunk.) She said most likely he's already settled over at Hendersons', ten miles to the southwest.

She also said she knows I'll be as good help all winter as I was this summer. She wants me to let Dad know I'm situated for the winter.

I'm not sure he'll even care.

SEPTEMBER 14, 1910

John and Karen have gone on an overnight visit to friends in the valley. Now's the time of year to go, with the haying done and the garden put up. Karen hasn't been anywhere all summer.

I am left in charge. There's not much to do except milk the cow, feed Karen's chickens, throw down hay for the horses, check the sheep in the lower meadow morning and evening.

3

The hard part is being alone, not hearing sounds of even one other person at work on the ranch. It's as though no one is left in the world but me.

I didn't like eating supper alone tonight. I don't like not seeing a lamp in the window over at the house now. It feels like John and Karen have died. What if they never come back?

John's sheepdog has come to sleep on the bunkhouse porch. She's been down making her rounds in the meadow. Maybe she knows I can use some company tonight.

Coyotes are howling up at the dump. I wonder if they'll eat the cow.

SEPTEMBER 15, 1910

Almost had a disaster this morning. Since there wasn't much to do after chores, I fired up the laundry tubs to do my wash. I figured things would dry fast on such a windy day.

Just as I threw my shirts into the rinse water and reached down to soap up the socks, a spark kicked from the fire under the tub and set ablaze a cluster of weeds. Before I could even move, the wind spread a pool of fire through the brush toward the house.

I could imagine John and Karen returning to a burned-out house. Like a madman I swung wet shirts at the flames. Back and forth between the tubs and the fire I raced, rewetting the shirts over and over.

I got it stopped just a few feet from the house. It took me an hour to pull myself together after that.

The rest of the afternoon I spent redoing the laundry in cold water, trying to get the scorch marks out of my shirts—and wondering if John would send me packing. I don't know why I didn't realize it was too dry to be building a fire on a windy day like this.

I thought of covering the burned ground with dirt before John got back. But after one shovelful I knew it would look as though I'd tried to hide something.

And then there was the smell of burnt brush.

John and Karen got back at suppertime. I could tell they were sniffing the air. I tried not to stammer when I reported what had happened. I was so nervous, though, I didn't talk loud enough and John said gruffly, "What are you saying?"

Finally I got it all out, and Karen said quickly, "I'm glad everything is all right, Sandy. I'm sure you've learned a valuable lesson."

Her eyes glanced toward the bunkhouse and I knew she was telling me to make myself scarce for a while.

I mumbled to John I was sorry and backed away till I could turn and hurry to my shelter here.

SEPTEMBER 16, 1910

This morning I asked Karen if John is going to fire me. She said unless my replacement happens along in the next day or two, probably not.

Maybe I should have gone back to Denver and started college. The tuition is paid, one year's worth, by the trust fund Grandma set up.

Last spring I was looking forward to going, even though I wasn't sure how I'd manage to study and continue working thirty hours a week for Dad and me to stay at the boardinghouse.

My brother, Doug, said I shouldn't concern myself

5

with Dad—that he wasn't worth it and I should do what was best for me.

Doug did what was best for him. He only had to work Saturdays to cover his lodging at the banker's house. He had time to study.

Doug liked college. I expect I would have, too.

SEPTEMBER 17, 1910

I'm having trouble sleeping, like I did when I first got here. When I close my eyes I see the dining room of a boardinghouse. Everything is agitated there.

The diners reach out to free a boy from the clutches of an angry man. There's a coffee stain on the man's trousers. He strikes the boy over and over.

Brown bitterness spills from the coffeepot in the boy's hand. His shirt strains across his back.

The insults the man spews in the boy's face—they're the same ones that followed me all the way from Denver, ricocheting from the walls of the empty cattle car as I traveled to Karen's.

But now, instead of insults, I hear a buzzing sound.

When I close my eyes and see the man humiliating the boy—me, his son—I hear a loud buzzing.

I wish writing it down could take it away forever.

SEPTEMBER 20, 1910

I've brought over a book from the house called *The Virginian*. It's about a cowboy in this part of the country. This will be the first winter since Grandma died that I've had a chance to read.

Karen has books from the year she taught school,

and John has some from the days when he camped out as a sheepherder.

In addition to reading, I'm going to write regularly in this journal. When Miss Langston gave it to me at graduation last spring she said journal keeping is a "meritorious way to organize thought and exercise writing skills—and especially to be recommended for those planning to attend college."

It doesn't seem very likely, but someday I could be going back to Denver to college.

SEPTEMBER 23, 1910

It's chilly tonight. I've got the blanket from Ed's bunk over my shoulders. It would feel good to have a fire in the Captain, but all the matches are up at the house. All the wood, too, except for a few scraps in the bottom of the box. At least in this kind of weather you don't have to strip and look for ticks anymore. Back in June, working with the sheep so much, I found two or three every night.

Karen wishes John would stay with sheep. They've been a good living. But there's no pride in sheep, she says. John's father was a cattleman and John's brother still is one, in the eastern part of the state. John won't be satisfied till he's a cattleman, too.

He has a few head now—forty or so—he's built up in the last three years. By year after next he hopes to have one hundred fifty head and no sheep.

I still haven't written Dad. Don't know what to say to him.

7

SEPTEMBER 25, 1910

Day after tomorrow John and I are going to the mountains for wood. We're to be gone three or four days.

John wanted me to stay home and do the chores, but Karen said the logging would be done quicker with two of us, and meanwhile, she was "perfectly capable of milking two cows and passing out some grain."

She'll leave the barn cleaning for us.

John said it was nice of her to take care of the front three-quarters and leave the back ends to us. Karen laughed and said she was glad the need to make soap gave her a good excuse to get out of the barn quickly.

I think John doesn't want to have me go along. He said, "It will be almost as fast—" but Karen interrupted him. I know he meant to say, "almost as fast if I do it alone."

As far as John's concerned, my staying's been a mistake. This summer when I worked with Ed, Ed said I was good help. John doesn't like me.

SEPTEMBER 26, 1910

I asked Karen why John doesn't like having me around.

She was chopping carrots and rutabagas for stew and didn't answer right away, as though she were trying to think what to say. She does that a lot with me, watches what she says to keep from hurting my feelings.

I appreciate her concern. But I'm not the same boy I was when I came in June. I'm not little and wounded and scared. In two months, I'll be seventeen. I've worked with men all summer. Things don't get to me like they used to.

Karen finally said that it takes John a while to warm up to people—especially someone who reminds him of his own youth, which was not a happy time for him.

She gave me an oniony pat on the cheek and said, "Stop worrying about it, Sandy. He's a good man with a kind heart—he'll come round."

I'm not so sure.

SEPTEMBER 27, 1910

Tonight we're at the logging camp, getting wood for winter. Camp isn't much more than a grassy clearing with piles of old horse droppings here and there.

John has made a shelter of pine boughs. It's tall enough so we can sit up and wide enough so we can lie down. One long side is open to the fire and the stars.

Karen sent along plenty of blankets and skins. She wanted John to take the hunting tent for warmth, but he said staring at all that white canvas would make him feel as if it'd snowed already.

When we started out this morning, John's sheepdog tried to follow the wagon. John made her stay.

"Need someone to take care of the place," he muttered.

I knew he'd rather have me back doing chores and his dog on the seat beside him. As though I had read his mind, he said, "I've sometimes thought of teaching that dog to saw wood."

I started to feel real bad then, but John looked at me

with a little smile around the edges of his mouth. He was teasing me. For the very first time, he was teasing.

I couldn't smile back for the aching inside me. Karen likes me because she's my cousin. But John doesn't have to like me.

We passed a little cemetery on the way to logging camp. I wanted to ask John who was buried there, but he seemed miles away in thought.

The cemetery is just a little corner of land with woods on two sides. It's fenced with unpainted pickets to keep out animals. There are no headstones like the cemetery Grandma's buried in, just crosses.

Grandma wouldn't have liked that, being marked with only a cross. Maybe that's why she had Doug pay for her headstone while she was still alive. She knew there'd be no money left for that kind of thing afterward.

At the same time she had Doug pay for his college and had the fund for me set up.

I remember how she cried when she told me what she'd arranged. She said when Grandpa was alive and owned the newspaper, they'd sent Dad to the best law school in the East. Now, look how little she was able to do!

I didn't know then that she was also crying for her house, which Dad was selling for debts. As I write here by the fire, I can almost smell her face powder. Her tears made trails through its fine, white dust.

I remember the feel of her paper-crisp hands on my cheeks as she lowered my head to her pillow the day she died.

"Sandy, dear, take a different road," she whispered.

"What road, Grandma?" I asked.

She looked toward the doorway where Dad had appeared. "A different one," she repeated.

John has turned in. I must, too.

SEPTEMBER 28, 1910

Worked from daybreak till dark today, stopping only for a cold lunch of meat and bread at noon. John and I didn't say much to each other.

At supper tonight, though, he said, "Not a bad day's work. Another day and a half should do it."

The way my shoulders and legs ache, I don't know if I can last another day and a half. It's good to know John was pleased.

For supper both last night and tonight we've had baked beans with ham chunks and hot biscuits. They cook all afternoon in a dirt-covered pit with a fire built over the top. When we come back at dark, we can smell supper cooking, and it's good—even with a little ash and dirt mixed in.

I hoped John would do some talking tonight. But he's just sitting there working his coffee cup with his hands and looking into the flames as though he's become a part of them, same as last night.

I'm glad I brought the journal. It's lonesome having someone here who isn't really here. Why doesn't he talk?

John has gone to bed. I got up my nerve to ask about the cemetery before he did. He was actually willing to talk! It's his father who's buried there—and three

11

babies, his and Karen's, that came too early—and some Lockridges from up the road.

I asked him if his father had come out to visit. He snapped his fingernail against his coffee cup and answered slowly. "You might say that. You might say he came out to see how I was doing. Died of tick fever. Bullheaded cattleman died of tick fever."

I nodded to let him know I was interested in what he was saying. It's not like talking with Karen, where you look right at her.

He said he and Karen warned his dad, just like they warned me, about needing to check for wood ticks in this part of the country. He said his dad must have picked one up down at the dipping vat. He hated sheep, but he'd been helping out "to show there were no bad feelings between us. . . ."

John turned his head away when he said that last part. It was as though he hadn't really meant to speak of it.

I already knew his father had ordered him off the family ranch when he was eighteen. Karen told me about it the first month I came, when I was still upset about Dad, and she was trying to make me feel better.

She said Mr. Hamilton, senior, didn't appreciate John's ideas. He told him if he knew so much about how to run a ranch, he could damn well start one of his own.

John rode the train to the other side of the state, which was as far away as his money would take him. Karen said he never went back, though once he did visit his mother and his married sister in Denver—which is where he met Karen.

I wonder if Dad cares about the bad feelings between him and me. Maybe I'm not writing to him because I doubt that he does.

John said his father was going to ship him out the start of a cattle herd. "Three yearling heifers and a young bull with promise." Karen had told him it wouldn't do to refuse them.

John gazed across the clearing as though he could see the cattle bedded there. He said his father had liked Karen. He'd only been here a few days when he said, "You got yourself a good woman, son."

Before John went to bed he dribbled the rest of his coffee into the ashes and mumbled, "Don't I know it."

I said nothing. Like the time Karen smoothed John's hair as he sat at the table and he reached up and grabbed her wrist, it seemed a private conversation not meant for me.

I went down to the creek to fill the coffeepot for breakfast.

Going to bed.

SEPTEMBER 29, 1910

I am still mad at John for treating me as though I were an idiot this morning. He thinks I purposely ignored his warning shout about a tree falling toward me. I am *not* stupid. I was limbing a tree and didn't hear him.

He had no cause to storm down the mountain cursing me. I was startled enough from having heard those branches crack against the earth twelve inches behind me. He could have asked if I was all right instead of grabbing my arm and swinging me around as if I were a ten-year-old kid with a rip in my coat.

He said to keep my mind with me if I was going to

13

work in the woods. I walked off and left him standing there. He's not my father.

After that I almost went down to the clearing for my things, thinking I'd walk back to the ranch. I knew he hadn't wanted me along from the very beginning. Finally, though, I decided not to give him the pleasure of being rid of me. I think he was surprised when I went down to help him snake logs back to camp with the horses.

He's been gone all afternoon now, taking a load to the ranch. Shadows are creeping down the mountainside. It's getting cold. I wish I were the one driving the load back. Karen said she'd cut out sheepskin mittens for me if she had time while we're away. I wonder what John is telling her.

When he left he said I should go on limbing trees and sawing them into lengths for the wagon. If I finished with that, I might try felling a tree or two as long as I watched what I was doing and didn't cut my "damn" foot off.

He didn't hear me mutter, "Damn your own foot."

I've finished with the work now and have the fire built up. Too bad it can only warm half of me at a time. The air was so cold early this morning that I woke up with my feet hurting.

It was the same kind of cold I used to feel in the Diamond Hotel where the snow blew in through cracks in the windows and the only heat was downstairs in the kitchen.

Thinking about the cold got me to thinking about Dad. All morning he leaned on my mind, causing me worry about his sleeping in alleyways now in freezing weather. I knew he couldn't still be at the boardinghouse. Not after the disturbance he made. Not without me there to work for our room and board. He'd go to Doug, of course. But Doug would do nothing for him.

When I was lopping off branches, I was really hoping Doug would at least put him up at the Diamond. I guess it's when I was remembering how bad the Diamond smelled that the tree almost fell on me.

I can't let thinking about Dad distract me like that.

I wish the wagon would come rattling up the trail long about now. There's nothing cooking in the pit. John must be planning to bring supper back with him.

John is here. He seems as glad to find me whole as I am to have him back.

SEPTEMBER 30, 1910

I am at the Lockridges' tonight, which I did not expect. It wasn't until we were breaking camp this afternoon that John told me the last load of logs always goes to Lockridges. Ed's the one who's always taken it, and since I was standing in for him . . .

I'm to saw, split, and stack the wood on the front porch. It will take two or three days. John thought I might "enjoy the ladies' company" up here. I didn't even acknowledge his remark. At the time, I thought I'd rather have been at the ranch talking with Karen than spending a couple of days with an almost-blind old lady I didn't even know and a twelve-year-old girl I'd only seen once.

The Lockridges live at the end of a road in the bottom of a small, bowl-shaped gulley that opens out of the mountains. There's just enough flat space for a barn, two corrals, and a turn-around in front of the house. The house is a small one with a long front porch and a creek to the side. There's a garden behind it.

When I got here, Joanna—the girl—was in the corral holding down a struggling sheep. An old dog was circling her and trying to bark at me at the same time. I had to shoo sheep away from a pole gate in order to get down the hill to the ranch.

I'd hardly pushed the gate open when a voice hollered, "Joanna, Joanna, the jam's a-burning!" A little woman no more than four feet tall had hurried out of the house onto the porch and stood there flapping her apron.

Joanna called back, "I can't come, Auntie Bea! Let it burn."

Aunt Bea kept working her apron and the dog set up a worse fuss. I wondered why in tarnation Joanna didn't let the sheep go and tend to the jam. It seemed I had to help Aunt Bea myself.

It turned out the horses were in a bigger hurry than I was. They'd smelled the barn. Despite my attempts to rein them in, they skittered down the hill with dirt flying up, me hollering, the logs thunking on the wagon frame, and the dog having a conniption.

I thought for sure we were going to run down Aunt Bea and plow over the house. Luckily, all that happened was we spilled a few logs. Once I got the wagon stopped, I sprinted past Aunt Bea, who had her hands clapped over her ears, and into the house to save the jam.

I might have saved it, too, if I'd thought to skim off the top half like we did when the potatoes boiled dry at the boardinghouse. The trouble is, I stirred it. I stirred that kettleful of carrot jam good.

Flecks of black scorch floated up through the whole batch. I don't know why I thought it would help to get the kettle off the range—it was too late to help— but I carried it out the back door and set it on a chopping block with hens scattering to get out of the way.

Aunt Bea said it would have burned without me anyway. But I felt bad just the same. She told me, "as soon as you help Joanna with that foolish ewe in the corral, I want to know about that ruckus you made driving in."

I like her already.

Joanna is very knowledgeable for a twelve-year-old. She'd been untangling a piece of barbwire from the sheep's leg. She had the wounds smeared with bag balm and was wrapping the leg by the time I got outside.

I've been given Joanna's room. She is sleeping with Aunt Bea tonight. Hot bricks are heating up the bed as I write.

Joanna told me the quilt on the bed was made for her by her mother. She thinks of her every night before she goes to sleep.

Though I didn't ask any questions, she told me her mother had died shortly after bearing her. Her father had been lost in a snow storm a few months earlier, and her mother didn't want to go on living without him.

I told Joanna I was sorry. It was as though she didn't want me to think any less of her because she has no parents.

17

I know how she feels.

It's too cold in this room to write any longer.

OCTOBER 1, 1910

It's good to be back in the bunkhouse where it's warm.

I left Joanna and Aunt Bea with a stack of wood two ricks deep all the way across the front porch and a woodbox filled to the brim.

I could have been back yesterday if I'd wanted to, but Aunt Bea and Joanna persuaded me to stay another day.

Joanna and I went riding in a meadow on the other side of the woods above the house. There's a little cabin there that Joanna's father built for her mother.

Joanna wanted me to see inside it. It's a bare place with just a stove, a table, and a rope-spring bed. It could use curtains at the window and a quilt on the bed, like at Karen's.

Sometimes in winter it's used by an old trapper named Zeke. In the fall, Joanna reads on the doorstoop while her sheep graze in the meadow.

"It's a nice little place, don't you think?" she said of the cabin.

"A nice little place," I repeated.

The horses were reluctant for us to gallop them bareback across the field, but we persisted. I can ride almost as well as she can, which, for a greenhorn from the city, isn't bad.

She said she hardly ever gets to ride because Aunt Bea's old mules don't allow such a thing.

I didn't tell her John would likely disapprove of my using his team for riding.

18

Dusk began to settle in as we herded the sheep through the woods and down the slope to the ranch where Joanna beds them away from bears and coyotes.

Someday Zeke is going to help her fence the meadow so she can leave the sheep up there with her dog for longer stretches during the day. There wasn't much need for fencing when Aunt Bea's husband ran cattle, since he grazed them on the public lands to the northwest.

Joanna says Uncle Albert wouldn't have approved of sheep on the place, but they're an easier way for her and Aunt Bea to make a living.

Joanna's built up a herd of thirty head from bum lambs John and the other ranchers give her. She bottle-feeds the orphan lambs till they can graze and sells off the wethers in the fall.

It makes me feel humble to think of all she does. She finds it curious how many things I don't know, but she never makes me feel stupid, the way John does.

When I left, Aunt Bea said she'd gotten used to Ed's bringing the wood, but I might do. She said in order to preserve the place, though, she'd have to give me driving lessons next time I came.

I hope she won't say anything to John.

OCTOBER 3, 1910

I've written Dad. Told him I'm at Karen's for the winter and I hope he's doing all right. It wasn't much of a letter. I could have told him more if I knew how he felt.

Once this summer when I sat under the willows down by the creek, I wondered if it even mattered to him that I had gone. Maybe he found someone else to take care of him, I thought. But I didn't believe it. More likely he was mad, mad as hell that I had left him to fend for himself.

I didn't want to write to him if he was angry. I didn't want it to seem as though I was writing because I was sorry for leaving him. I'm not sorry.

I hope he will answer. Karen is having me send the letter to her sister Martha with a note requesting Martha's help in locating him.

I had to explain to Karen about not sending it through Doug—he doesn't want anything to do with Dad.

OCTOBER 5, 1910

I am reading *A Tale of Two Cities*, which Joanna insisted I take home. It was her father's favorite book, and hers, too. She's proud of the two shelves full of books that belonged to her father.

Some are schoolbooks like the New National Readers that her Uncle Albert taught her father and, later, Joanna from. There are volumes of Emerson's essays and the complete works of Dickens and Shakespeare. There are other classics, too, and some popular novels.

Joanna said she and Karen trade books all the time, except now they've both read most of what they have.

The last night I was at Lockridges', Aunt Bea asked me to read aloud from Whittier. She likes poetry. Also music. She had Joanna play Uncle Albert's violin for us.

The E string was missing and it sounded out of tune, but both Joanna and Aunt Bea were pleased with the songs Joanna's taught herself.

It seemed strange to see a girl play the violin in a

worn-out dress that doesn't fit well and a pair of boots that gave up long ago. The Lockridges don't put much stock in clothes, but they sure like books.

OCTOBER 8, 1910

I have some tea steeping on the Captain and another hour left till bedtime. Been sawing up wood for the bunkhouse. I'll split it as I need it.

I've found violin strings in a Sears Roebuck catalog that was under the washstand. Twelve cents plus two cents postage for an E string. I'm going to send away for one for Joanna.

Someone has folded over the corners of the pages in the catalog that have women modeling long under-wear. I wonder if Karen wears that. It says, "especially adapted to older women who must have warm under-wear the year round."

None of the women in the pictures are old, though. They look like Miss Tyler, from school last year. Nice shapes.

I might order myself a razor while I'm at it. There's an army one for $1.50 or I can get a complete shaving set with strop, shaving brush, hand-engraved alumi-num shaving mug, cake of soap, and straight-edge razor for $1.79.

OCTOBER 10, 1910

Butchering this week. A cow, three yearling lambs. Two hogs left to go. If I don't think about what I'm handling, I can haul the fresh meat over my shoulder to the ice house in the hillside.

I'm trying to be good help to John, but I have been

21

sick twice watching him gut the animals. We don't talk much. If Karen cooked the entrails, like some people do, I know I couldn't eat them.

I don't think John likes butchering, either. If I were a rancher, I wonder if I could get someone else to do it. At Joanna's, a neighbor hays the meadows for half the crop.

John has pegged the cowhide in the creek so the hairs will work loose with the current. He makes good-looking chair backs and seats with cleaned skins.

OCTOBER 17, 1910

Snow! Not a lot. But enough to quiet Wyoming. When I awoke this morning, the stillness was so complete, it seemed as though sound had been turned off like electric lights in a Denver power failure.

When I stepped out for breakfast, gray grasses and browning meadows had all been salted with white. The air seemed clearer, as though it had been filtered by the snow. In the timberline the dark green of pines rose out of the whiteness. As if to let me know some things hadn't changed, a horse snorted in the corral.

More of the cattle, who've been grazing all summer in the public lands to the southwest, showed up this afternoon. They've been drifting down from the mountains with the cold weather.

The sheep have been feeding in the fields close to the ranch since haying finished.

OCTOBER 18, 1910

Karen says it would be better to order a whole set of violin strings for Joanna since if one has worn out, the others are likely soon to follow. I've decided to also buy her a pitch pipe to tune the violin with.

Karen says I need to be thinking about winter clothing. The sleeves on Doug's corduroy coat that I've worn for three years end closer to my elbows than my wrists, and it pulls across the back.

I have fifty-five dollars in wages for the summer (after paying Karen back five dollars for the shoes I had to have in August). Though Dad has seen fifty-five dollars go in and out of his hands many times in one night gambling at the faro tables, I've never had that much money in my life.

Next summer maybe I can earn closer to forty dollars a month, like Ed, since I've had some experience.

I'm going to buy "the famous lumbermen's King-sheep-lined duck coat with wombat fur collar" from the new fall catalog. It looks like the one John has. $5.75. I wish I had it now.

Karen says the order will take about three weeks to get here if I ride down to the post office tomorrow to send it. I don't like to have to spend $3.33 on rubber work boots, but I guess it's better than having wet feet when I'm out for very long. I'm ordering two pair of long johns and a pair of pants.

Having all those things come at once will be like getting school clothes, back when Grandma was alive. I wonder if I should order a harmonica. I could teach myself to play in the evenings.

No, that's enough stuff for now.

With postage, it all comes to $19.85. Three months' wages sure go in a hurry. Still, I have remaining a whole lot more than I had when I left Denver.

OCTOBER 20, 1910

Dad should have my letter by now. If he wrote as soon as he got it, I should be hearing from him any day.

OCTOBER 22, 1910

Karen isn't feeling well, at least not in the mornings. The other day when I went over for breakfast no one was up. I started the fire in the range and was about to put the coffee pot on, when Karen squealed in the bedroom.

My face turned hot. I felt like I shouldn't be in the house. John came out of the bedroom just as I was leaving. He didn't look annoyed to see me as I would've expected. In fact, he looked pleased with himself.

I felt even more embarrassed.

"You and I will be getting our own breakfast for a while," he said as he washed in the icy water from the kitchen pump. "Karen's needing extra rest in the mornings."

He didn't seem at all concerned. In fact, he actually hummed as he sliced the bacon. Karen looks fine to me when we come in to midday dinner.

OCTOBER 25, 1910

John rode out this afternoon to check on the last of the cattle. Since the snow has melted, the stragglers have headed back into the hills on the other side of the ranch.

24

It was good to sit at the kitchen table alone with Karen. We talked about Aunt Bea and Joanna—how real Joanna's parents are to her though she never knew them. And also about what Joanna would do if anything happened to Aunt Bea.

Karen said Aunt Bea is healthy enough that she'll be around for many years to come, but that Joanna would always be welcome here with her and John.

Karen had finished my mittens and I had to try them on to satisfy her. I could tell she was pleased that I liked them.

It's the first time anyone has made something for me. I thought of the time she spent cutting them out while John and I were in the woods. And then the hours of stitching by hand through the fleece and leather, since it's too thick to go through her sewing machine.

You have to care about someone to go to all that trouble.

She wanted to know if I minded being in the bunkhouse by myself. I told her I was comfortable there. She laughed when I told her that I take my tea to bed and try to balance the cup with one hand while I write in my journal with the other. I have to keep leaning over to dip my pen in the ink which I set on the chair, and all with a blanket slipping off my shoulders like an old woman's shawl.

I didn't tell her how lonesome it is some nights. How I get to feeling like I belong to no one. Back in Denver, it might be late at night, but Dad always came home to me.

If he didn't, I went looking for him. Not that I ever found him, but at least I knew he hadn't stumbled on the way back, that he wasn't lying cold and drunk in some alley. He would never say where he was on those nights, just that it was none of my "damn business."

I checked the streets anyway.

Here, I have no one to check on.

I wish I hadn't read *Tale of Two Cities* so quickly. It was a good book and I liked to imagine I was sitting around the fire at Joanna's, reading it out loud to her and Aunt Bea.

OCTOBER 28, 1910

Karen has just been here! The way she pounded on the door, I thought it was John. I thought something was wrong. She hardly gave me time to pull on my pants before she came in.

She glanced over the room and I felt ashamed of the picture someone had tacked on the wall of a young woman stepping out of her petticoats. If I'd known Karen was coming, I'd have taken it down and swept the floor. I'd have hung up my clothes.

She raised one eyebrow at me, then let me off the hook by saying, "Just like a bunkhouse."

I pulled my clothes off the chair and set it in front of the stove for her, but she shook her head. Said she'd only be a minute. She'd been wondering, after I mentioned Joanna and her parents, whether I had any mementos of my own mother.

I said I hadn't.

She took from her pocket a little leather-covered box.

26

Inside it, on a delicate chain, lay a golden arch with a small, tear-shaped purple stone suspended from its center. Two tiny diamonds were set into either end of the arch.

Karen lifted my hand to receive it, and the cool metal of the chain curled in my palm. "This belonged to your mother," she said. "It was given to me by your father when I graduated from high school. You are the one who should have it, as a remembrance."

She paused as though she thought I would have something to say.

But I didn't. The necklace had no sudden meaning for me. It was hard to imagine it had ever come from Dad's hand or touched my mother's neck. It wasn't something that had been made for me, like Joanna's quilt had been made for her.

I took the box and returned the necklace to it. Setting it on the washstand, I thanked Karen. She couldn't know that her mittens mean more to me than a piece of jewelry intended for someone else.

How odd it felt to be standing so near her. I hadn't realized I'm that much taller than she is. Maybe I have grown since I came.

I watched her glance again about the bunkhouse and wondered at how much I love her. Not only does she care about me, she accepts me.

I drew my arm around her shoulder and rested my chin in her hair for a moment. She gave me a quick squeeze around the waist.

From the door I watched her cross the road and disappear into the house.

I wonder if she's ever sorry she married John. There are times when he doesn't speak to her or to anyone else. What would she do if something happened to him?

Would ten years be too much difference between us? Do cousins ever marry? I am going to bed. I wish she'd kept the necklace. I already have the mittens.

OCTOBER 30, 1910

Things have slowed down around here now that the wood is in and the butchering done. Not much to do after chores. I can see why John doesn't keep extra hands on.

I like being able to read by the Captain after dinner and again before bed, but am beginning to feel like a mole. No one's passed by in weeks.

I wonder if I'll be here this time next year. I wouldn't mind seeing a moving picture long about now. Just riding down Market Street on the trolley would seem exciting.

NOVEMBER 1, 1910

I asked Karen today if she ever misses Denver. She said, "Sometimes." She says after six years she's gotten used to the solitude of Wyoming, but even now, she wouldn't mind some lively conversation and fresh sugar cookies in her sister's kitchen or going window shopping with John's sister.

She says whenever she's gotten cabin fever she's thought of the two years John and his herding partner lived crammed in a sheep wagon with no other company for months at a time.

After dinner she stirred up a double batch of sugar

cookies and told me it's too early in the season for cabin fever.

No letter yet.

NOVEMBER 4, 1910

A Mrs. Donneville was here today with her two little girls to visit Karen. She smiles too much, like that teacher I had in fourth grade who always praised us in front of the principal. Once the door was closed she would rap our knuckles with a ruler for the smallest offenses—even the girls.

I rigged up a swing in the haymow for the little girls. They looked at me shyly under their long eyelashes and wanted me to push them. The older one asked if I lived in the bunkhouse. The little one wanted to know if "Mrs. Sandy" was getting dinner for me.

At dinner Mrs. Donneville studied me from across the table and looked in a knowing way at Karen.

She said, "Sandy won't be safe at the dance. Not after Christine sees him."

The little girls giggled. They were snuggled on either side of me like guards protecting property. They had already told me about their aunt Christine—Mrs. Donneville's youngest sister—who's eighteen.

My ears turned warm. John left the table soon after. He seemed to prefer his own company in the tool shed to Mrs. Donneville's.

At the end of the month Mrs. Donneville's other sister is marrying one of the Hendersons. There's to be a dance at the hall to celebrate. We are all invited. I hope Ed will be there, too.

The little girls hugged me good-bye when I lifted

them into the wagon. Mrs. Donneville smiled at me as though she knew something I didn't. She said to Karen she'd "send Daniel over with the shoes next week." Then she chucked the horses and was off, with the girls waving over the side.

I must have looked suspicious. Karen pressed the end of my nose and said, "The shoes are not for you, dear. They're some Mrs. Donneville no longer uses that might do for Joanna to wear to the dance."

It's good they're thinking about shoes for Joanna, but why aren't they concerned about a dress? Her dress will show even more than shoes.

After supper Karen asked my opinion on some cloth she wants to make up for the dance. When I asked her why she didn't just wear the yellow dress she went visiting in this fall, she got exasperated and said I was "just like John."

I sighed and told her that of the two pieces of cloth she was considering, the golden brown looked friendly, while the blue with small white flowers looked to be for someone sort of delicate.

She raised her eyebrows as though that were an odd thing to say. I shrugged. I may not know *much* about dresses, but I do know Karen has enough of them, and Joanna doesn't.

NOVEMBER 7, 1910

Tomorrow is the eighth. My birthday. I told Karen I'll ride down to the post office after dinner. I have a feeling there'll be a letter from Dad. Probably there won't be. But maybe there will.

Last year he forgot my birthday altogether. But the

year before, he took me out for a phosphate at the soda fountain.

Seventeen is an important birthday. A boy's not a kid anymore. He's looking out for himself. He has his future to consider.

A father should remember his son turning seventeen.

NOVEMBER 8, 1910

Karen's the first one to bake me a cake since Grandma died. She's not the best cook, but she made a three-layer applesauce cake with nuts and raisins and a caramel icing that you could have served to the Governor. Even John was impressed. He and I had a second piece that left us groaning with stomach aches.

Better than the cake, even, is this heavy flannel shirt Karen sewed for me. It's got to be better than any of the shirts in the catalog. The shoulders are roomy and the sleeves plenty long, which is more than I can say for my other two.

Karen says that the yellow plaid with brown and blue lines in it makes me look "warm and friendly." She says not to get it dirty, so I can wear it to the dance.

So I guess I've got to leave it hang for two weeks.

John, too, had a present for me—a brown felt hat that a hired hand left behind. John said he'd been waiting for just the right person to give it to. The crown is not too stubby and not too tall. I'm surprised he gave it to me. I like it a whole lot.

Karen suggested I wait till tomorrow to go for the mail, since the wind was picking up and it looked like snow. We still haven't had anything more than a few flurries.

It's only an hour down and an hour back to the post office, so I wasn't worried any, but John said I'd better wait and go in the morning.

"Heck, it's only two o'clock," I said. "I'll be fine."

Karen pressed her lips together in that way she has of asking me not to argue. Usually she does it out of concern I'll aggravate John.

But John and I haven't had any problems for many days, and he didn't seem inclined toward any then.

I was confused. I was impatient to be gone. I needed to see if Dad had written. Since Karen's waiting for a catalog order same as I am, I started to say something about that.

She looked so distressed, though, almost as if she didn't *want* me to get a letter, or maybe thought there wouldn't *be* one, that I shut my mouth. I was kicking inside to be gone, but I sat back down at the table and tried not to look how I felt—angry.

Tonight after supper John dealt me into a game of gin rummy with him and Karen. I could have appreciated his friendliness more if it weren't that I'm getting uneasy.

This afternoon I thought it was important to hear from Dad on the exact day of my birthday. But I guess I won't kick as long as there's a letter tomorrow.

Maybe it won't be what I'm expecting. Maybe there won't be one at all. If that's the case, better I don't know till after my birthday. I guess.

NOVEMBER 9, 1910

There's something for me. It's not from Dad.

Ten dollars with a note saying, "Happy Birthday,

32

Sandy—Doug." That's all. That's *all*! Not one word about Dad. Not one single word. Hasn't he even seen him?! Why doesn't he say? He knows I'll be worried. Doesn't he care? *Where is Dad?!*

Karen has just been here with a letter from her sister Martha. *News of Dad.* I don't know what to do. Return to Denver or stay where I am.

From Martha—

    . . . Not wishing to entrust Sandy's letter to anyone, I went myself to the bank where Douglas works. He was most relieved to have news of his brother. However, when I produced Sandy's letter for their father, Douglas wished to have nothing to do with delivering it.

    I sensed that he has had a good deal of trouble with his father. He said that he is currently boarding him at the Diamond Hotel down on Market Street.

    I can't tell you how disagreeable that part of town is. I took Tom with me and we entered the hotel, which does not even maintain a front desk. The parlors were closed off, and from the smell of things the place is occupied by derelicts and drunkards. . . .

    At last, in the kitchen, we found a man peeling potatoes. He said yes, Mr. Mannix did reside there, but that he wouldn't be in any shape at that hour (eleven in the morning) to receive guests.

    Though I was reluctant to turn Sandy's letter over to a stranger, I finally agreed to leave it with the cook's helper who assured me that Mr. Mannix took his dinner in the dining room every day and that the letter could be delivered to him that very afternoon at table. . . .

Greetings to Sandy. I hope ranch life agrees with him. . . .

The Diamond. I told Karen it's a terrible place to live. It's the absolute least Doug could have done for Dad. I told her if Doug's not even checking on Dad, I'd better go back.

She wants me to stay. She said with a roof over Dad's head and one meal a day, he can survive on his own. She said if people kept taking care of him, making him comfortable, he'd never make the effort to stop drinking. He would never change.

He doesn't change. In the four years I've looked after him, he has never changed.

Karen said I have my own life to live now and Dad has his. She stoked the Captain before she left and took away the supper she'd brought over. I didn't feel like eating.

The wind is picking up. It makes the fire spit and snap. There'll be a wind in Denver, too. A cold wind that makes the curtains snap away from the windows in the Diamond.

Dad won't think to put the curtains on the bed for warmth; he won't even bother to get under the covers. He'll lie in his coat on the valley-shaped mattress with his shoes still on his feet. The Diamond may be better than an alley, but he could still freeze to death there.

I wonder how long it would take in winter to get to the train in Rock Springs. When I came in June, I was two days walking that distance. Where would I sleep now, with snow on the ground?

I am tired. I feel as though I've lived a hundred years.

NOVEMBER 11, 1910

I am, for now, going to stay. It would not be right to leave Karen and John without a hired man. Ed could not quit his job at Hendersons' to come back.

But if Dad should fall sick or suffer an accident, I will have to leave. I cannot count on Doug.

When I showed Doug's message to Karen last night, she was sympathetic. With Doug! As though he doesn't have things just the way he wants them.

How will I know if Dad does all right—that is what worries me. Tomorrow I will post an order for a quilt from the catalog. I will have it sent directly to Dad at the Diamond. At least he will be a little warmer, if he thinks to use it.

I won't say anything to Karen about it. She says I need to let Dad take responsibility for himself.

I don't think he ever will.

NOVEMBER 12, 1910

Does Dad's not writing mean he doesn't think of me at all?

NOVEMBER 13, 1910

John showed me how to sharpen blades on the grindstone today. At dinner he said I did such a good job on the ax, he ought to be able to fell a tree with one swing. I think he's trying to make me feel better.

Karen wants me to ride up to Joanna's the end of the week to tell her about the dance. I wish the violin strings were here.

NOVEMBER 14, 1910

I have written Martha in Denver to ask if she will telephone the Diamond from time to time to inquire after Dad.

When I left in June, I meant it to be a punishment to Dad. Why do I still care?

Another thing I've been wondering about: What a person does today—can it change everything he's done before?

Say a man told someone in his son's presence that he was proud of his son, that he was a fine boy.

Then the man later said in front of other people his son was worthless, lazy, stupid. Would what the man said the second time cancel what he said before?

Which would be the way the man really felt? Would he have changed his mind? Would he change his mind without a good reason?

Could the man be confused? How would the son know what to believe?

NOVEMBER 15, 1910

John said it would snow tonight and he is right. It's not just snowing, though. The way the wind's howling, this could be a blizzard. There's a fierce draft coming in around the window, but if I hang a blanket over it, I won't be able to see the snow.

Joanna's father was only twenty when he died in that blizzard. I read it on the marker in the cemetery on my way back from Lockridges'.

He was just a little more than three years older than I am. Joanna's mother was seventeen. Died at seventeen. Her name was Anna. His name was Joseph. Jo-anna.

They were not married—didn't have the same last name.

I should stuff the sand roll against the door and put a few more sticks in the Captain for the night, but I don't want to put my feet on the icy floor. If Karen or John get up in the night, they will wonder why my light is still on.

Karen will worry that I have fallen asleep with the lamp too close to the bed.

At Grandma's house I used to like to watch the snow fall outside the window at night. I liked to hear the wind shrink itself as it passed between the houses.

I felt warm and cared for—safe.

Now the wind means something else to me. It means not everything is warm and cared for.

NOVEMBER 16, 1910

Tonight I think of my mother. Buried in Boston, or so Doug told me.

I don't remember her.

When I was four or five, I liked to think she had only gone away on a long journey. That someday I would run up the steps to Grandma's house where we had always lived and find her sitting in the parlor waiting for me.

One day I even asked Dad at the parlor door, "Where is Mother?"

37

That was a long time ago, but I'll always remember the stricken look he turned on me—as though I had pronounced a curse.

After a long silence when my question seemed lost even to me, he answered, "Dead." The flatness of his voice and his exit from the room shattered my daydream.

It wasn't until I was eight and attended a funeral that I spoke again of Mother. At the graveside I asked Doug where she was buried. Then I wanted to know why they had buried her in Boston.

"Because she died there," he said. "Now hush."

Hush. That is what Grandma always said when I asked about Mother. One time, though, she said, with her head twitching like a pecking chicken's, "Your mother should never have gone back to Boston. Better still, she should never have left it in the first place!"

I remember a Christmas before Grandma stopped inviting guests to dinner. Dad came to the table loudly cheerful and unsteady on his feet. While the others ate their dinner in silence he carried on one-sided conversations with Doug and me.

Afterwards I found Grandma in the kitchen quivering with anger. She said to one of the woman guests, "His wife ruined him. Just ruined him!"

Someday I'll ask Karen what she knows about my mother.

NOVEMBER 17, 1910

To Joanna and Aunt Bea's today. Beautiful day for a ride. Eight inches more of snow. All the fence posts are capped with it, and the pine trees wear puffy white gowns. On such a clear day all that brightness makes a person squint.

My passage on Karen's saddle horse, Sue-Babe, was the first to be recorded on Lockridges' road—except for a few rabbit tracks. I could hear Joanna's sheep bleating even before I got to the gate. John says sheep are noisy when everything is fine. It's when there's trouble that they turn stupid as stones.

The ranch looked like it had been tucked into a comforter of snow for the winter. The sheep moved around the slopes like small, black-faced snowdrifts.

Joanna was as excited about the snow as I. She was also glad to see me. Nothing would do but for us to tramp out a fox-and-geese circle in the garden where the snow was still untrammeled.

We chased each other round and round the circle and down the paths through the center until we finally fell laughing into the snow. Like overturned turtles, we lay on our backs, gasping for breath. I flapped my arms in a snow angel. Joanna did the same.

It wasn't till then I noticed she had no mittens. Her hands were scarlet with cold. She thought I was silly to be concerned, but we went inside just the same.

Aunt Bea had Joanna change her stockings and me put on a pair of dry socks from Uncle Albert's drawer. She wanted to know what I'd been up to.

I told her I was waiting for a letter from Dad, though I didn't really expect him to write. I don't know why I said that. It's not as though I wanted to talk about it.

It was just the way Aunt Bea sat there counting with a finger the stitches on the knitting needle, looking like she was really interested in me. She wanted to know if

Dad was expecting me back for the winter. I told her no. I'd already written and said I was staying.

I put on my new hat for her to see. She said I looked "mighty fine," though with her eyesight, I'm not sure she can tell.

Then I had to tell her and Joanna about the Henderson wedding and Karen expecting them to come down for the dance and spend the night. Karen had sent a package up with me without saying what was in it.

I was as surprised as Aunt Bea and Joanna when it turned out to be that blue cloth with white flowers made up into a dress for Joanna. She was really pleased.

But when she was backing toward the bedroom to try it on, she had a fearful look like she half expected the dress to be taken from her. I know what that look was. It was a longing. A longing not just for clothes like that dress, but for the people who usually give a person clothes. A mother. A father.

Every year after Grandma died, Doug brought me a box of clothes. They were not new. Some were not even Doug's. They allowed me to go to school without shame, but not without hurt. I wanted Dad to have given me those clothes, Dad to have seen my need, Dad to have cared.

That dress changed Joanna. Or is it only that I saw her differently when she had it on? It made her look older. Her braids still hung like woven wheat over her shoulders, but she didn't look like a shapeless child anymore. She had a waist like a young woman's.

Her brown eyes seemed darker and her cheekbones showed. Even her wide mouth seemed to fit her better. She was almost pretty.

40

I showed her where the dress should be hemmed, according to what I've seen in the catalog. I had dinner up there, too—of course. Aunt Bea asked me to "come give an old woman a kiss on the cheek" before I left. She said Joe never used to leave without a kiss for her.

When I obliged and put my arm around her shoulders, she sighed—not in a contented way, but in a very sad one.

Joanna insisted on seeing me off and stood shivering in her wet shoes while I cinched Sue-Babe. She tied her dress bundle on the back of the saddle and repeated what I was to say to Karen about how pleased she was with the dress and what time she and Aunt Bea would be down on the day of the dance.

From the saddle I looked down on her huddled in a worn-out coat that must have been her uncle's with her faded dress hanging out at the bottom and her shoes splitting at the toes. I ruffled her hair and said I hoped Aunt Bea was knitting her a cap.

She grinned and pulled a hand from under her arm where she had tucked it for warmth to wave good-bye.

NOVEMBER 18, 1910

John is riding over to Donnevilles' tomorrow to get a file set Mr. Donneville is slow in returning and to ask about the shoes for Joanna. Mostly he's going for the shoes. Karen says Charlotte Donneville is long on promises and short on carrying them out.

I told her I could have ordered Joanna some shoes when I sent off my catalog order. John seemed surprised I would do such a thing. I don't think much of someone who would forget Joanna needs shoes.

41

Karen is as pleased that Joanna liked the dress as Joanna was herself. She keeps wanting to know how Joanna looked in it.

I tell her, "Good."

That makes her exasperated. She says, "Is that ALL?" She wants Joanna to have a dress with style. Says Joanna's old enough to notice that sort of thing now. "Didn't it—?"

"You'll see," I tell her. I don't mind having her worry a little over it, just like I worried not knowing Joanna was going to get a dress. After all, Karen could have told me she was making it so I wouldn't have been so fussed.

Not that I really minded. Karen wanted me to be surprised, too. For some reason, though, I don't want to discuss what that dress does to Joanna.

Going for the mail tomorrow.

NOVEMBER 19, 1910

No letter. Maybe Dad's not well.

John got the shoes. Mrs. Donneville had changed her mind about giving them away. It's only because her husband, who was feeling guilty about John's tools, nudged her along that she finally handed them over. John says he won't soon forget that woman. Neither will I.

NOVEMBER 23, 1910

The catalog order was in today, and I'm not sure it's a good thing. My face looks like chicken scratching and it stings to boot. Either I'm a clumsy oaf or that new razor is as dull as the edge of a plate. It's a good thing the dance is still three days away. I hate to go over to the house for breakfast tomorrow.

If John laughs, I'm likely to punch him. I hope no hairs grow till after the dance so I don't have to try this again.

My new coat is here. It looks dandy. Feels like a man's coat, not a scrunched boy's. New pants, new work boots—this is something to wait for.

I've been working on my shoes, treating the leather, polishing them up. Karen hinted that I wasn't taking very good care of them, letting them get wet and then drying them out too close to the fire. I've got oil on them now for waterproofing.

I wonder if Joanna ever proofs her shoes. She should have some rubber work boots, too. Her strings and pitch pipe are here. I hope she's going to like them.

Karen's cutting John's and my hair tomorrow. I'm looking pretty shaggy. The day after that John and I have to stay away from the house except at dinner time because Karen says "the ladies" (she, Joanna, and Aunt Bea) are going to bathe and beautify themselves.

We'll have a late dinner in place of supper and then have a light supper around eleven o'clock at the dance, Karen says. I told her I don't remember anything from Miss Luellyn's dance class that Grandma made me go to when I was eleven.

Karen thought that was very funny. She said half the people in Denver, including herself, had suffered at Miss Luellyn's. She said not to worry about the dancing part. Those who don't already know how learn very quickly, because no one's allowed to sit out. I don't know about this.

It sounded exciting at first. A chance to be around people for a change. I didn't know I'd ever miss being around people. People going by me on the street. People talking on the corners, on the school yard, in the shops.

It does get lonesome out here. It will be good to hear people talking again. But I don't know about that dancing.

NOVEMBER 26, 1910 *Noon*

I have had a long soak in the tub pushed close to the Captain and feel like a new man. It seems a shame to crawl back into my work clothes, but I don't want to do chores in my good ones. John had his bath over here while I was shoveling out the barn. He didn't want to be caught bathing over at the house by Aunt Bea and Joanna.

They arrived little over an hour ago, Joanna bareheaded and with her fingers nearly froze. Aunt Bea was all bundled into blankets and skins in the back of their rickety old wagon. John and I hauled her out like a sack of potatoes.

It took them two and a half hours to get down here with that balky pair of mismatched mules they have. Karen is reviving Aunt Bea and heating bath water for all the ladies.

John dug out an old razor for me yesterday and showed me how to strop it. He said the one I bought is good enough for scraping window panes and that's about it. If I use plenty of soap and keep the strokes short and smooth, I might keep from carving up my face, he says. I appreciate him not laughing. Karen did, though.

She's been hoping it would snow again so we could take the bobsled to the dance. As it is, there are too many bare patches so we will shake along in the wagon instead.

I've got it filled with clean straw, and we'll put hot rocks in and some bearskin robes. John may let me spell him on the driver's seat. The dance hall is right next to the post office, the only buildings in the middle of nowhere.

NOVEMBER 26, 1910

It is after midnight. The lamps have gone out over at the house. I couldn't sleep if I wanted to and have fed the Captain another round of wood.

Mrs. Donneville's sister sure is pretty. She has a woman's shape, poufy in the chest and narrow at the waist. A shape I could feel when she pressed against me dancing.

Mrs. Donneville introduced us in her voice that's falsely sweet. "Sandy, dear, this is Christine."

Christine smiled and offered me her hand. For a moment I touched her long fingers that smelled of lotion. Then I looked at the floor.

She had on stylish, soft-leather shoes. So did Mrs. Donneville. Not at all like the serviceable ones I'd polished for Joanna.

Mrs. Donneville's feet moved away.

45

Christine said, "What's the news from Denver these days?"

I thought she was referring to Dad. My neck, my scalp, my whole face burned. I wondered what Karen had told Mrs. Donneville and Mrs. Donneville told Christine about Dad and me.

I couldn't think what to answer. I stared at Christine's hair, which was piled in soft rolls on her head. She went on to talk about a zoo they were planning to add to the amusement park at Lopen Gardens in Denver.

Joanna couldn't have understood how grateful I was that she tugged on my arm and said the squares were forming, she wanted to show me how "Cinder Belly" went.

Christine waved good-bye with an amused smile. It made me feel as though I were Joanna's age.

The evening passed quickly. There were far more men than ladies, but I never seemed to have a moment's rest. Arms pushed and pulled me this way and that, dancers laughing and whooping as they spun past me.

Every so often a slow dance was played. Christine would appear at my side and lead me onto the dance floor. She'd move up close and lace her fingers through mine. I had trouble remembering which foot to lead with. By the third time, though, I began to enjoy it. All night I had a desire to reach over and feel her hair.

She talked a lot, saying nothing I remember much, except for, "Are you planning to file on land soon?"

"I haven't decided yet," I said, though in fact I haven't even thought of it. She said there was a nice parcel next to Charlotte's—but there wasn't any water on it.

If I had someone to talk to here in the bunkhouse, I wouldn't have to write all this down.

At ten o'clock food was laid out on boards for a stand-up supper. It wasn't until then, as people milled about with plates in their hands, that I realized I hadn't seen Ed.

I went to Aunt Bea, who told me he'd been left in charge at the Hendersons'. I was ready to go home after that. I'd counted on Ed's being there. I wanted him to see me in my new clothes, ordered in men's sizes. I wanted him to see how I was keeping an eye on Aunt Bea and Joanna like he does.

I guess I wanted him to think when he saw me that I wasn't a kid anymore—that I was worth his having given up his bunk at Karen and John's for.

When the dishes were cleared away, Joanna joined Aunt Bea and me and announced that the last dance of the evening I must save for her since everyone else had already had their turns. I agreed.

During supper I'd seen her chatting merrily, with a man's arm around her shoulder. I wondered who he was. I also wondered how many dances she'd been to. She seemed much more at ease than I and never lacked for partners, either.

I'd overheard someone say she was blossoming into quite a young lady. Karen had helped her pin her braids up in a flat spiral on either side of her head. She looked sweet and sort of delicate.

I watched her be swept away by a mangy-looking sheepherder fellow. Then I was dragged off by Mrs. Donneville herself. It's a good thing the dance was a fast one with changing partners. I didn't seem to have time to answer her questions about Christine and "little Joanna."

It was late when the head fiddler announced, "Last dance. Find your lady and waltz her good-night."

Joanna was beside me in a flash. I slipped my arm around her shoulder and said it was good to see her. Karen passed by following John. "Having a good time?" she called. We waved in answer.

It turned out I didn't actually dance with Joanna, though. Christine squeezed in between us. She told Joanna Mr. Carson was hoping to dance with her. I remember Joanna glancing at me with a look I didn't know the meaning of. She said quietly that she was going to dance with me.

Somehow, though, I ended up with Christine, and Joanna with the sheepherder. Christine told me not to worry, that he and Joanna were old friends.

When someone turned the lamps down, halfway through the dance, Christine put her head on my shoulder. I drew my arm snugly around her waist.

It was a very nice dance.

I'm going to bed.

NOVEMBER 27, 1910 *Morning*

I am in trouble. Bad trouble. A guy could use a friend to talk to long about now. This morning when I came down the ladder from the loft after pitching hay to the mules, Joanna was standing in the doorway.

She had her hands thrust into the pockets of that big old coat she wears, and her braids were still up in coils over her ears, which does make her look older. She told me I didn't have to feed her mules. She was coming out to feed them herself.

I told her I didn't mind, and hoping to make a joke, I added, "You can take care of the other end." Without a word she took a shovel from the wall and went to work cleaning the stalls.

Not knowing what else to say, I shrugged and went out for the milk cows. They, at least, were their own selves.

While I was milking, Joanna came and stood behind me. As soon as the pinging of the milk streams on the bottom of the pail gentled into a steady swish-swish, I asked her if she'd had a good time at the dance.

She said most of the time. I was pretty certain then what the problem was, but I wasn't sure what to do about it. She came out from behind me and stood on the other side of Bessy. Kind of wistfully she said, "Christine sure looked pretty last night."

"You looked good yourself," I told her. I watched her hand move along Bessy's backbone above my head.

"Christine dances real well, too," she said. I admitted she did. Then she asked if I liked Christine much. Now how was I supposed to answer that question? I didn't even know myself. And if I did, I probably wouldn't tell Joanna.

I finally asked if it mattered to her if I did. She didn't answer. One moment she was looking at me, her eyes turning wet, and the next she was gone.

By the time I stumbled over the milk stool and hurried after her, she was through the barn and halfway to the house. She didn't turn around when I called to her. To top things off, Bessy put her foot in the milk

49

before I got back. I swore and gave that animal a whack that sent her plowing out into the corral.

Picking up the overturned bucket, I walked outside and flung it as far over the fence as I could.

Now I sit alone in the bunkhouse in the middle of the morning with no notion of what to do. I'd been looking forward to Joanna's being here. I'd thought we might ride the horses and that she'd like to swing in the haymow.

That won't happen now. Maybe she's too young to understand how it is when a guy's seventeen. Maybe I don't understand, either.

She can't go away upset. Dinner will be ready soon, and after dinner she will be heading back up the hill. What can I do? Already I've curried the mules. I've gone over her wagon tightening bolts, and tied a gunny sack of straw on the seat to soften the jolting. What else. . . .

More than enough has happened for one day. If I don't set it down, I may burst.

When no one called me for dinner, I began to think they were all seated at the table enjoying their meal without me. Finally I stuffed the violin strings and pitch pipe in my coat pocket and stalked over.

When I pushed open the door Aunt Bea said, "Here he is!" The house was warm and moist from cooking and smelled of seasoned roast and berry pie cooling. Karen was at the stove making gravy and looked at me oddly, as though to ask what was going on.

Joanna paused for a moment at the sink, then returned to mashing the potatoes with vigor. John I could hear rummaging around in the bedroom.

"Looks like the weather will hold till you get home," I said to Aunt Bea.

"Is there snow coming?" she asked.

"Probably not," I said lamely.

Dinner could have been straw for all I enjoyed of it. Joanna would not look at me. Not even when I took a big spoonful of the carrot jam she'd brought Karen. There were no flecks of scorch in it; she'd made a whole new batch.

Aunt Bea remarked on how quiet we were and said she seemed to have held up better than the young people. Karen exchanged looks with John.

There wasn't much talk after that, and I felt lower and lower, knowing it was because of me. When Karen served the pie, Joanna poured coffee and was careful not to brush against my arm.

John asked Aunt Bea to stay, and she said she'd like to but she couldn't trust Zeke in her kitchen. They laughed, and I felt so out of place that I got up and stacked the pie dishes.

John said he'd hitch up the mules. I told him to stay put—I'd do it. I was feeling desperate by then. It seemed Joanna planned never to speak to me or even notice me again. As I took down my coat, Aunt Bea said, "You go along, too, Joanna-girl. Make sure Sandy gets those mules hitched to the right end of the wagon."

I could have kissed Aunt Bea! Slowly Joanna took her coat from the peg and went out ahead of me while I held open the door. Our shoes crunched on the frozen dirt as we walked side by side, but not together, down to the barn.

Without waiting for me, Joanna slid back the barn

door just as she'd be doing at home a few hours later. I stepped past her into the dimness and wheeled around. She lowered her head and stepped aside.

I tried to say something. All I could manage was, "Joanna."

Her eyes were awash in tears. I reached for her hands. They were small and calloused. With my thumbs I caressed scratches and felt over the stubby fingers.

She pulled away from me and with a little choking sound said, "My hands will never be like Christine's— not in my whole life!" She ran down the aisle toward the mules.

I was stunned. Too stunned to follow. Not until I felt the steps of a mule behind me did I face her.

With a halter rope in hand, Joanna seemed sure of herself again. She looked at me steadfastly, no smile on her face. Everything had not been forgotten.

"I am sorry about that dance," I said.

She tilted her head in acknowledgment. As she passed by she let the sleeve of her coat brush against me.

NOVEMBER 28, 1910

John did the chores alone last night. Karen had me imprisoned in the house. She was upset about Joanna. She said what I chose to think and do about Christine was my business, but she wouldn't permit me to be careless with Joanna.

I reached for my hat and said I would be more considerate in the future. Karen wasn't done with me yet, though. She said Joanna is old enough to form affections, being almost thirteen, and that she's apt to be more easily hurt than other girls who've been around people more.

I didn't want to talk about it. I said I wasn't looking for a sweetheart, but I'd keep what she said in mind. She looked at me fiercely. *Some* people my age were looking not only for a sweetheart, she said, but a husband.

I felt my face grow warm.

There seemed more she wanted to say, but I didn't give her any encouragement. Already she'd told me more about my situation than I wanted anyone to know.

NOVEMBER 29, 1910

I'm afraid to tell Karen I promised to go to Lockridges' for Christmas Eve supper and stay the night. She'll likely call that "encouraging Joanna."

It's almost as though I can't be friends with her. Karen thinks she'll come to like me so much she's bound to be hurt later. Hurt by what? By my moving away? By my having other friends? I can't promise not to do those things. That would be like planning to marry her!

Maybe Karen has an answer to all this. Some things I'd like to find out for myself, though.

I hope Joanna is pleased with the strings and pitch pipe. I told her not to look in her pocket till halfway home.

DECEMBER 2, 1910

Winter has settled in. Night before last we had a blizzard with winds to send us halfway into Colorado. Maybe that's why I didn't sleep so well—I was thinking of Colorado. Wondering if the quilt has gotten to Dad.

Thinking he can't spend the rest of his life at the

53

Diamond. Worrying how unlikely it seems he can ever go back to being a lawyer.

I sure hope Doug will have someone check in on him. It makes me nervous to have no news.

DECEMBER 4, 1910

John and I are establishing a winter routine. He milks mornings, I milk at night. While he chops the ice free in the water troughs and the creek in the corral, I shovel out the barn and put down clean straw.

After breakfast we load the hay sled from a stack in the field and drive along the creek bed pitching the hay to the cattle. The sheep are fed up by the barn.

John is starting to go over the machinery, fixing things that barely made it through haying season, and putting things in order for next spring's plowing. He doesn't seem to mind my company in the machine shed.

I'd like to learn all I can in case I ever have a ranch of my own. Karen says John had his eye on this place when he used to herd the Hendersons' sheep through here. He used to worry someone would claim it before he was able to.

I could file a claim. The law says a person has to be twenty-one. But people don't worry about that. John said the best land's taken, but there are still some half-way decent pieces farther north.

When John moved onto his land he had enough sheep from working shares with the Hendersons to start right in ranching. Karen was telling me about it one night at supper.

She said the buildings went up one each season with

John doing the work himself, except for hiring a Norwegian builder—the best he could find—to put up the little house he brought Karen to when they were married.

I think it made John feel good to hear her tell about his accomplishments. Karen's good at that—talking a person up in front of other people to make him feel worthwhile.

She laughed when she described the sheep wagon John lived in for two years. She said the day they moved into the house, John took the tin roof off the wagon and burned the wagon to the ground.

John shook his head. "I still don't have any more room than I did in the wagon," he said, with as close to a smile as he ever gets.

How different John is from Karen. Quiet and serious while she is almost always cheerful and talkative. I don't know if it's a good thing to be so different.

Marrying someone more like oneself seems a better idea. I think it would be easier to understand each other.

I wonder if I will ever have a place of my own.

DECEMBER 5, 1910

There's going to be a baby on this ranch after all. At least maybe there is. One's due to come the end of May. Karen wouldn't have told me if I hadn't walked in on her going through baby clothes this morning.

She said she doesn't like to talk about it until she's more certain things are coming along all right. She was so pleased and hopeful, I couldn't help putting my arm around her.

"It's got to work out one of these times," I said, giving her shoulder a squeeze.

"Yes, one of these times," she said quietly.

It seemed like maybe I'd said the wrong thing.

As I took John's work gloves out to him in the barn, I remembered what he'd said about not keeping any ewe who bears a dead lamb two years in a row.

Did that mean the ewe would always have dead lambs or did it mean John couldn't afford to wait to find out? I debated about asking him and finally decided I didn't really want to know.

Maybe it's different for women than it is for sheep. But maybe it's not, and I guess I don't want to think about Karen not getting something she's got her heart set on.

DECEMBER 7, 1910

I'm making up my mind early not to expect to hear from Dad for Christmas. I don't want that ruining everything. He's not going to write, and I've got to get used to it.

I'm not even going to look through the mail at the post office. I'll just take it home to Karen each time and if there's ever anything for me, she can bring it over.

DECEMBER 9, 1910

Karen has a packet of Christmas letters to mail to friends in Denver. I've written a line to Doug and one to Dad. I'm asking Dad if he got the quilt and saying I hope he's doing all right, same as last time. I'm telling

Doug thanks for the birthday money and asking how Dad is.

I hope Doug will invite him to Christmas Eve supper. Last year Dad did well even with the in-laws there. I was proud of him. He and I were even invited to join everyone for a program at the church afterward.

Dad said it was better, though, to leave while we were ahead. On the trolley home a group of carolers with lighted candles came aboard singing, "Why lies he i-n such mean estate, where ox and la-amb are feeding?"

Dad said he'd never heard that carol before, but he liked it. When the chorus was repeated, he put his arm around my shoulder and joined in, "Whom shepherds gua-ard and angels sing."

We didn't need Doug and his in-laws. We had each other. I hope Doug'll remember Dad doesn't have me this year.

DECEMBER 12, 1910

Karen is making a hat for Joanna for Christmas. I asked her to. It is to be of sheepskin with a fleece-lined cuff that can be pulled down over the ears or folded back.

Karen thought Joanna should have a scarf, but I think she needs a warm hat. We cut a paper pattern and pinned it together to get a proper fit. I am going to make the mittens that will match.

There's a piece of sheepskin left, and I'm buying it from Karen. I didn't tell her it's to make a muff for her for Christmas. I think it will be easy to stitch the ends together into a cylinder with the fleece on the inside to keep her hands warm. I'll attach a leather string so she can hang it from her neck like the catalog shows.

DECEMBER 14, 1910

Karen has been letting me do my laundry in the kitchen since it's too cold outside and is much easier to heat enough water on the range than it is on the Captain.

I still bathe in the bunkhouse, but the water's always lukewarm and there's not much of it. One teakettleful of hot water can't do much to warm a tub of cold.

I have my wet laundry hanging on a line across the room. Karen has some sheets frozen like boards on the lines in the other half of the bunkhouse.

It smells clean and damp in here.

DECEMBER 15, 1910

No wonder Karen wasn't eager to make a sheepskin cap. It's much harder to work with leather than I expected. Karen has waxed the thread, but it still requires a thimble to force the needle in and a pair of pliers to pull it out.

I am using a block of wood to push the needle against, since the thimble's too small for my fingers. I can see now how long it took Karen to make my mittens.

What can I do for John for Christmas?

It didn't seem this morning when I helped John take apart the rake in the machine shed that anything unusual would come of today. I wasn't expecting to ride in Donneville's new sleigh with the curved runners, and I wasn't expecting to get a letter.

Christine came by on her way to the post office with the little girls. She asked if I'd like to come along. I shouldn't have gone. Something made me hesitate, and I shouldn't have gone. But the little girls were so eager and Christine so fetching— My heart pumped twice as fast as it usually does. John said to suit myself when I went in to tell him where I was off to.

Christine knows how to handle horses, but she drove too fast. The harness bells jingled wildly and the little girls clung to the side of the sleigh. They weren't very happy about sitting on the other side of Christine, away from me.

When we got near the post office Christine urged the horses on even faster, as though she were trying to impress whoever's horse was tied up outside. It turned out to be her new brother-in-law.

She forgot all about me. So did the girls. They went to look at the candies and hair ribbons in the shop Mrs. Stewart keeps in one corner of the post office. I wondered what I was doing there at all. I'd been trying not to pay any attention to the mail. I didn't even want to ask for it.

When Christine reached for a letter Mrs. Stewart (without my asking) held out to me, though, I had to take it.

Christine cooed, "Sandy must have a lady friend."

I glanced at the return address and thrust the envelope into my coat as I headed out the door. Martha in Denver. She would be writing only if she had news of Dad. I had a feeling, a powerful feeling, that the news was bad.

I wanted to get home. I wanted to be alone.

Christine asked me to drive on the way back. She laid her head on my shoulder and invited me for Christmas Eve supper at Donnevilles'. She had asked her brother-in-law to come with her sister, and of course she would ask Karen and John.

When I told her I had other plans and refused to change them, she seemed hardly able to believe such a thing. She took the reins and did not speak the rest of the way.

As soon as she dropped me off, she goaded the horses into a sudden trot that made the sleigh sweep from the yard, runner squeaking on the snow and bells jangling furiously.

Only the little girls waved good-bye.

It was clear to me the person I had most enjoyed dancing with was *not* the one I preferred to be with at Christmas.

Karen was amused. She had set extra places at the dinner table. She said she and John preferred to spend a quiet Christmas Eve at home anyway.

John said he could bet I had been the sole purpose for the party. I thought Karen would be upset that I planned to go to Aunt Bea and Joanna's. I'd put off telling her about it. She was surprised, but didn't say anything.

On and on I write, as though this were an ordinary day.

As though there were not an unopened letter at my feet on the bed. I am afraid to read it. Afraid I should have gone back to Denver, afraid I will go back to Denver now.

MARTHA'S LETTER

December 9, 1910

Dear Sandy,

It is with deepest regret that I write to tell you your father is dead. Having suffered a fall down a flight of stairs late on the evening of November 28th, he did not regain consciousness and died in the hospital at noon the following day.

By the time Douglas was traced, it was imperative the burial be conducted without further delay, thus you were not sent for.

Douglas has come to me, distraught at the prospect of telling you. Whether he feared you would blame him or blame yourself, was not clear to me. I offered to write you now, with Douglas writing when he is more composed.

Your father had apparently been visiting a woman he had known for some years. She turned him out shortly before midnight and was unaware of the accident that transpired on his leaving the building. She told Douglas they had been drinking.

There is no will, according to Douglas, and no property to be disposed of—which you no doubt are already aware of.

I hope you will always consider yourself welcome at my house, as I know you must also be at your brother's.

With sincerest sympathy,
Martha Thompson

61

DECEMBER 18, 1910

I should have—

DECEMBER 19, 1910

"Sandy, you are not yourself," Karen says.
 I shake my head.

DECEMBER 20, 1910

"I don't think it's Christine that's on your mind,"
Karen persists. "What is wrong, Sandy?"
 What can I tell her? She meant well, convincing me
to stay. She meant well, but she didn't know Dad like I
know Dad. He needed me. I turned my back, just like
Doug, when he needed me. Now he is dead.

DECEMBER 22, 1910

Two days till Joanna's. Karen reminded me I must not
encourage affections when I don't know what my
plans for the future are.
 Plans. She expects me to be making plans. To be
thinking of the future. Not to stay on here. She thinks
I don't need her.
 Why don't I have plans?

DECEMBER 24, 1910 *Noon*

Cleaned out the tack room for John for Christmas.
 "You might make a rancher after all," Karen said,
"or at least a good housekeeper."

I could not smile.

She is worried.

John was quiet when he saw the tack room. Made me uneasy. I had changed everything around.

He finally said, "Takes a man with ideas to get somewhere in the world, Sandy. Thank you."

Karen said she'll treasure always the muff I made her. Told John he'd have to take her out in the bobsled so she could try it out.

I'm to open my presents when I get back. That way Karen can be sure I'll *come* back, she said. I don't know how to tell her what is on my mind. I want her to know, but I don't want to talk about it.

DECEMBER 24, 1910 *Midnight*

Christmas Eve. I must write. The house still smells of roast goose with sage dressing and mince-apple pie Joanna cooked for dinner. It is comforting to be here. But part of me has been plowed up tonight and may never heal.

I came at dusk. Joanna was in the barn, milking early on account of my coming. Had her braids tied up in loops the way Karen showed her.

She asked if I was hungry, then fired a stream of milk at my chin and laughed. It made me want to cry. I was startled. Then she was so concerned by my seriousness, I wanted to kiss her.

She lit a lantern and hung it on the post beside me as I milked the other cow. I never wanted to finish.

We ate on a tablecloth Aunt Bea's mother wove for Aunt Bea's wedding fifty years ago. It'd been darned many times, but looked as white as fresh snow.

Afterward, I went up to check on Zeke, whom Aunt Bea had been expecting for dinner. Joanna had told me he sometimes didn't like to be around people. She'd wanted to come along.

But it was cold and I hadn't been ready then to give her the hat and mittens. I asked if she'd tune up the violin instead.

No one answered at Zeke's. The cabin was dark, but smoke twisted from its chimney. When I opened the door a familiar smell swept from the cabin. A disgustingly familiar, musty smell. In the lantern light, I saw on the table an empty, overturned bottle of Jimmy Brown whiskey.

Anger spread through me. It seemed to creep up the back of my neck and grip my mind.

Inside I found Zeke—a grizzled old man—lying on top of the covers in his long underwear. Spit dribbled from his mouth as he wheezed and snorted in his sleep. The stench of him made my head reel. I found myself opening and closing my fists.

I wanted to kill that drunken man. I wanted to grab him by the neck and shake him as though he were my father. I wanted to scream, look what you've done to yourself! Look what you did to me! Never a letter. Never an apology. Never a sign you cared if I lived or died.

Zeke moaning in his sleep reminded me he was not Dad. Nonetheless, I heard Dad's shouts rise in my head. "Clumsy, no-good imbecile! Worthless excuse of a son!" There was no buzzing in my ears then. Rank, whiskey air filled my lungs. I heard the coffeepot clang on the boardinghouse floor—the women scream—chair legs scrape— Mrs. Logan hollering, "Mannix! You put that kid down!"

I remembered breaking free of Dad's grip. Stumbling down the hall to the street, his words flying after me. They pierced the back of my head like arrows. "That boy has never been anything but trouble! He's like his goddamn mother—goddamn money-grubbing leech! Let go of me, you sons of bitches!"

There in Zeke's cabin I shook like a quaking aspen. It helped to open the stove door and shove in more wood.

The last time I saw Dad he was flat on his back in bed, fully dressed and reeking of whiskey. I had no fear he'd awaken when I gathered my few things together, stuffing them into the pillowcase from the upper bunk.

I stood over him for a moment before I left. "Enjoy your rest," I muttered. "Tomorrow Mrs. Logan will have you thrown out on your ear, and I won't be there to help you up!"

I didn't even cover him.

Tonight I faced Zeke and eased him under the covers. I told myself I would never be like him. Never.

I heard the notes of Joanna's violin drawing me home when I hurried back through the woods. I wanted to be safe in the front room with her and Aunt Bea. I wanted to forget Dad. Forget I'd ever had a father.

The music changed to a Christmas carol. It reminded me of Denver and the trolley. Of carolers singing a shepherd chorus. It brought back Dad's voice, "Whom shepherds guard and angels sing—" His arm circled my shoulders. We'd had each other.

Something inside me crumbled. I leaned against a tree and buried my face in my sleeve. All the words Dad and I would never say—all the things we had never done together. . . .

There is nothing left to wait for. Dad hasn't written and he's not going to.

DECEMBER 25, 1910

Joanna knows. Told her before I left. I wanted her to understand why I had not been myself.

She touched me on the shoulder. Touched me as though we were old and trusted friends. My eyes swam.

Before I could turn away, she thrust her arms around my waist. "Sandy, I am sorry," she said.

I rested my chin on her head, then pulled away.

DECEMBER 26, 1910

Karen wants to give me a tonic. Says I don't look well. She knows it's not my health, but isn't prying.

DECEMBER 27, 1910

I have a woolen muffler from Karen for Christmas. From John, a three-pound hammer. "A declaration of independence," he called it. Allows you to not only put things together, but take things apart. Can't build a life of your own without it. So he said.

JANUARY 4, 1911

John to the post office today. Karen over with a letter from Martha. "I wish you had let me know," was all she said.
    Flannel shirt and three pair of socks from Doug. No letter.

JANUARY 6, 1911

More snow.

JANUARY 7, 1911

John is saddling his horse to take birthday greetings to Joanna. I feel like going nowhere.

JANUARY 9, 1911

Went to Big Creek to cut ice for the cellar next to the bunkhouse. Wind so cold my feet will never thaw.
    John never complains.

JANUARY 11, 1911

Karen says Dad's death was the natural outcome of the way he chose to live and had nothing to do with me, just as John can't be held responsible for his father dying of tick fever.
    She doesn't understand.

JANUARY 16, 1911

Helped John haul manure from the corrals to the pastures for spreading. When the ground thaws in spring, he wants irrigation ditches dug for more alfalfa.

JANUARY 17, 1911

I don't want to go back to Denver. Ever.

JANUARY 18, 1911

Karen says again it's not my fault Dad died and I've got to let it go.
    He *wouldn't* have died if I'd gone back to Denver.

JANUARY 19, 1911

In Denver this time of year the snow lies heaped in the gutters tinted with coal dust. In Wyoming it lies thick in the gulleys, thin on the fields with last year's stubble poking up through it.
    Winter lasts too long wherever I am.

JANUARY 21, 1911

Calving season coming up. John says he'll need my help.

JANUARY 23, 1911

I know Karen has more to say. I appreciate her not saying it.

JANUARY 25, 1911

A warm chinook blew last night. Uncovered an ugly ground that can't begin to green for two more months.

JANUARY 26, 1911

John's got me building onto the calving sheds on the south side of the barn.

He said this morning that a father's dying can keep a person down. He said it helps to walk back through the stubble and reclaim the moments, however few, when you felt you were in your father's favor.

I can't seem to walk backward or forward. I can't even walk around.

FEBRUARY 1, 1911

Karen says reading late into the night every night is not good for me.

It's better than bad dreams.

FEBRUARY 2, 1911

More snow. Winter will not end.

FEBRUARY 5, 1911

I need to be making plans. Didn't Karen tell me that? I don't seem able to think. It's as though my head is hollow.

FEBRUARY 8, 1911

Scorched my socks drying them too close to the Captain last night. Bunkhouse smells terrible.

FEBRUARY 10, 1911

Calving heifers have been moved into the pasture next to the bunkhouse. I'm to check them before I turn in at night.

FEBRUARY 12, 1911

Been thinking about my mother. Maybe she isn't dead like people told me. Maybe they said that to keep me from asking questions.

It's a dumb thought. A seventeen-year-old doesn't need a mother. I guess.

FEBRUARY 13, 1911

More snow. Wind.

FEBRUARY 14, 1911

I've taken out the necklace again. Fingered the stones and felt along the chain—hoping it would put me in touch with my mother.
    It didn't. I can't remember her at all.
    I need to talk to Karen.

FEBRUARY 16, 1911

Dad and Mother were seldom happy together. That's what Karen says. There are many things she's wanted

70

to tell me. Things she thought would help me understand the situation with Dad. Things I might someday want to talk to Doug about.

She started back at the beginning. Back when Dad was born, twenty years after his brother—Karen's father. Grandma treated the new baby as though he were a crown prince, Karen says.

Grandpa was busy with his newspaper office. He didn't realize till much later that his son needed a firmer hand than he got from Grandma.

When Dad was ready for college, Grandpa decided it was time for him to develop responsibility as well as prepare for a profession. That's why he was sent to law school back East.

Grandma was "desolate" with him gone.

Grandpa died during Dad's last year at college. Karen remembers the carriages, draped in black, rolling past the house to the cemetery. Grandma was upset Dad didn't come home for the funeral. But she proudly told everyone he was in the middle of examinations at school.

Six months later Dad returned to Denver with a wife. Grandma was furious. She felt deceived and called Mother "conniving." Said she had tricked Dad into marrying her to get his money.

Grandma was not about to give up her son, Karen said. She persuaded Dad to move into the big house. There she could "take care of him properly" and "keep an eye on 'that woman.'"

She treated Mother with less regard than if Mother had been a parlor maid. That's what Karen's mother said.

Karen said we'll talk again tomorrow. John came in to suffer the removal of a sliver from under his nail.

71

Karen says I was "a precious baby." That Doug was shy and preferred to sit by the stove where he drew little attention, but I was "sweet and observant."

I wish she could have told me my parents felt the same. But she didn't. She said she doesn't know how I could have been a happy baby coming from such an unhappy home.

Mother often escaped to Karen and Martha's house with Doug and me. Sometimes she would sit at the kitchen table and say nothing. Other times she would cry and Karen and Martha would be shooed from the room.

Finally she would talk—of wanting to see her parents, of not understanding Grandma's meanness to her, of being lonely in the evenings when Dad stayed out politicking.

It's true what Grandma once told me about Dad running for lieutenant-governor. But it's unlikely, Karen says, that Dad lost because of "purchased" votes.

After the defeat he grew reckless. Didn't go to his law office for days at a time. Grandma complained that he spent less and less time at home. She blamed it on Mother.

Karen didn't want to tell me what happened after that, like she wanted to soften it somehow. But there was no way around it. I told her I needed the truth.

She said Mother was encouraged by Karen's parents to make a trip back East to lift her spirits. Karen says Mother's face would come alive when she talked about stepping off the train with Doug and me.

She talked about what bedrooms we would sleep in

at her parents' house and how she would dress Doug and me to show us off to her friends. We were to be gone two months.

Dad pouted. He wouldn't take Mother to the station. Karen's mother had to find a neighbor to do it. She thought Mother would be well justified in never coming back. That thought also occurred to Grandma.

She convinced Dad to hurry to the station and get Doug and me if he ever hoped to see us again. Karen's mother was waving good-bye to us from the platform when Dad appeared and boarded the train.

In a flash he whisked Doug and me down the steps and turned to thrust Mother, who was struggling to reach us, back into the car. He jumped from the train as the wheels began to turn.

Karen says her mother jerked me—who squalled with fright—and Doug, who stood there in shock, back from the rails and called frantically to a conductor to stop the train.

The train went on, though. Dad collected us and went home. The ticket agent told Karen's mother that the engineer could let Mother off at the nearest town and she could have the signal put out to be picked up by the evening train on its return to Denver.

Karen's family met the incoming train, but Mother was not on it. She never answered the letters Karen's mother wrote telling about Doug and me.

It was feared she had thrown herself from the train. Karen's father suspected Dad had told her on the train he was divorcing her.

Months later Karen's parents received a newspaper clipping reporting Mother's death in Boston.

I've told Karen there is nothing more I need to

know. It's enough that one of us—Doug—remembers whatever else there is.

FEBRUARY 18, 1911

My feelings about Dad are all a jumble again. What kind of person was he? Did he never think of someone besides himself?

Doug turned his back on him, told him no many times when Dad and I needed a place to stay. He'd take me in, but not Dad.

But a person doesn't throw his family away like that, does he? Maybe Dad was not the man he should be, but . . . but he was our dad.

The drinking and gambling—those could have been defects he had little control over. And maybe the self-ishness, too. Maybe it was all Grandma's fault.

John says he doesn't keep a calf or lamb from un-distinguished parents. He fattens it and sends it to the packing plant. He knows it's unlikely it will turn out better than its parents.

Will I be like my father?

FEBRUARY 22, 1911

Calves are starting to drop. Sheep in a few weeks. John and I are taking turns getting up at night. Three live births. One dead.

FEBRUARY 23, 1911

Did Dad take advantage of me like he did Grandma? Maybe he could have controlled the drinking and gambling. Maybe he could have thought more about his wife and children.

If anyone ruined Dad, it wasn't Mother. It had to have been Dad himself—and maybe Grandma for making it easy for him.

And maybe me, for picking up where Grandma left off.

FEBRUARY 26, 1911

Helped John pull a calf tonight. Heifer couldn't push it out. I thought it was dead when we finally dropped it, but John had me grab a hind leg, with him taking the other, and we swung it up and down to clear its lungs.

It started to breathe! It actually started to breathe.

Those little creatures have the softest fur on the top of their heads.

FEBRUARY 27, 1911

John says he thinks a city person *can* run a ranch, but he also said he's seen enough of them fail. Mostly because they thought they knew much more than they actually did.

But a halfway smart person who's willing to learn—who will look around and listen—has as good a chance as many country-born ranchers.

The best thing, he says, is to spend a couple of years learning on someone else's ranch.

I could do that.

John and I nursed a little calf here by the Captain this morning. It was born so close to the creek it slid right onto the ice and broke through. It was half froze to death when John heard the mother making a fuss and went down to investigate.

We rubbed him dry with gunny sacks here in the bunkhouse and wrapped him in a canvas to keep him from losing more heat.

He was so still for a couple of hours that John thought he was a goner. I kept trying to force warm milk from a bottle down him, to fortify him from the inside, but he wasn't interested.

John said I might as well come up to dinner since the calf wasn't going anywhere. I noticed the little fellow's legs beginning to jerk, though, so I brought my dinner back to the bunkhouse.

Well, the calf was on its feet, peeing in front of my bed when I got back. I was one nervous father trying to lure that little rascal away from the Captain before he got burned.

Once I got him outside he frisked about as though he were filled with popping corn. John was as pleased as I was and went for the mother.

We weren't at all sure she'd take the calf this long afterward, but she was a calm thing who didn't make any objections. Not jumpy like her son!

John says an animal's temperament isn't necessarily passed on like its physical characteristics, just as with people.

Karen has said that John is a little like his father—but not altogether like him.

Doug is not at all like Dad. He never touches liquor and is cautious with his money. He's also quiet.

Maybe I'm not like Dad, either.

MARCH 8, 1911

Four more heifers to go and the sheep are coming on any day.

MARCH 12, 1911

This morning when I was pitching hay down from the loft, I discovered a baby's cradle way back under the eaves. It hung like a little pine monument between two carved end pieces.

It could have been taken apart and stored flat, but instead it had been placed there just as it would have if it still held a baby. I ran my hands along its polished sides in the dusty barn light. John put it there, I'm sure. It must have been either he or Ed who carved it.

What makes a man and woman want so badly to bring a child to life? Why is there a stirring in me when I see life come to a newborn calf?

Cows grieve when their calves are taken from them. Did my mother grieve that much more for me?

Would a parent grieve for grown children, too?

MARCH 16, 1911

Two lambs last night. One an orphan. More snow coming in.

MARCH 20, 1911

A letter from Doug reminding me of Grandma's
money credited for a year of college. Saying Dad is
buried next to Grandma and Grandpa in a plot
Grandma had paid for.

I feared all along that the quilt never arrived, but
Doug said he found an almost-new one in Dad's room.
He gave it to someone he figured needed it at the
hotel. I would have done the same.

He says he's got Dad's shaving kit—wondered if I
might want it someday.

And a picture of the three of us trying to play base-
ball when I was five and Doug was ten.

A picture of Mother he'd like to keep.

And two letters from me. One of them delivered too
late, one coming apart at the folds.

MARCH 21, 1911

Dad resting on my mind.

MARCH 22, 1911

Last winter Dad and I saw a Frenchman fly the first
airplane in Colorado. Dad could have gone to see the
flight alone. That wouldn't have bothered him any.

But he waited for me while I finished my chores at
the boardinghouse, and we ran for the trolley that was
carrying half of Denver to Overland Park.

I won't forget the box-kite airplane with snow spray-
ing from its propeller. And I'm not going to forget that
Dad waited for me.   ·

Four o'clock. John has ridden out for Mrs. Henderson. The wind has picked up. The snow is drifting. Can hardly see across to the house. Now, with the light beginning to fail . . .

The baby is coming, too early to survive. With the trouble Karen's had before, John wants Mrs. Henderson here. I told him I'd ride over for her—that he's the one who should be here if Karen gives birth before Mrs. Henderson can get back.

He did not want to leave Karen. He did not want to send me out with a storm closing in. Finally he decided he could not risk my losing the way, both for my own sake and for Karen's. He's been gone three hours now.

In good weather he knows the land between here and Hendersons' like he knows his kitchen table. But in a storm where he can't see ten feet around him? Joanna's father lost his way in a storm.

If Ed were here, he'd have gone, and John could have stayed.

Five-thirty

I return from my rounds. Am warming myself by the Captain. Checked in on Karen, then the ewes—number 13, who won't let her lamb nurse unless I knee her against the pen, and 43 and 28, who are coming on fast. Then back to Karen.

She wants to be alone.

I want to be alone, too, but I have been put in charge of the ranch. I must be there if she needs help before John comes.

79

When I found her crying this afternoon in the kitchen with her hands on her side, she did not want me near her. I had rushed toward her. I was alarmed by her paleness and the strange way she breathed—as though she were in pain.

She thrust out her hands. She told me not to touch her. Not to come another step! She wanted John!

I stared at her. It was as though she didn't know me. As though she had forgotten who I was—I, the boy she told on her wedding day to come and spend a summer with her on the ranch as soon as I was old enough. Me—Sandy—who's talked out all his problems with her.

I would have thought she'd call me if something were wrong, that she'd know she could depend on me to help in any way. I never expected her to speak to me sharply—to send me away without explanation.

Six-thirty

I write because I am nervous. Suppertime and John still isn't back. I lit the lamps for Karen. She's lying on the sofa in the front room where it's warm. Doesn't want anything to eat. I've brought back a saucepan and a can of beans to heat on the Captain.

Karen's been crying again. When I went in she called out, thinking I was John coming at last.

"It's just me—Sandy," I said. "Is the baby coming?"

She shook her head and looked away from me.

"Can I bring you something?"

All she wanted was a drink of water. I told her I'd knock twice next time to let her know it was me.

Damn, I wish John would get back.

Eight o'clock

Milking's done. Number 43 restless and dilating, but no lamb yet. Number 28 lying down. Fed Orphan and the bum lamb born last night.

Karen's dozing, I think. I didn't go inside, just listened at the door this time. Maybe like me with Martha's letter, she needs to be alone with her sorrow awhile.

I shouldn't mind her having been sharp with me. She's got a worry on her mind. Maybe Dad, too, was worried when he yelled at me in the boardinghouse. A person can't see into someone else's mind to know. I'm trying not to believe she thinks of me as useless or too much a kid to have been of help to her.

All I do know is, if she'd been speaking to a man—to Ed—she would not have been so harsh. I've been doing a man's work for almost a year and she still does not see me as one.

Nine-fifteen

John should have been back hours ago. Karen is worried. Will take *Tale of Two Cities* over. Maybe she'd want me to read to her.

Ten o'clock

John and Mrs. Henderson have come. Going to bed. Have the one A.M. lamb watch.

MARCH 26, 1911

In a couple of days I am going to see Joanna. I need to get away, be with someone who's glad to see me come. John agreed to my taking the bum lambs up to her. The baby still hasn't come. Karen is in good hands, given circumstances.

I regret giving up the lambs, especially the one I've been hand-feeding for a week—Orphan. I'd secretly hoped John would give him to me.

But thinking of Joanna this morning, I knew it was right that she should have them. She has two people to support—herself and Aunt Bea. Any help John and the neighbors can give her is well directed and much appreciated.

If I want sheep of my own, I can buy them. It has occurred to me clearly, for the first time, that I have no one but myself to support now. Not that I have been supporting anyone for the past nine months, but I felt I should have been.

Now I have only myself to worry about.

I've thought of starting a small herd of sheep—buying from John, grazing on his place in exchange for work. The way he feels about sheep, though, he may not want to see any on the place once he sells his own off.

MARCH 27, 1911

Mrs. Henderson left this noon. No birth. Karen's labor pains have slowed to twitches. Mrs. Henderson says bed rest might save the situation. Not a few days, she says, but a few months. No lifting, no being on her feet for Karen. It's the only thing Mrs. Henderson can recommend. She says few women will stay quiet that long, but maybe few women want a baby as badly as Karen.

I am awkward around her. The way she spoke to me still makes me feel puny. I've got to keep my eyes on the bigger picture. Try not to think of that one time with Karen as a measure of how she regards me. Seven new lambs.

MARCH 28, 1911

I thought John was at the house getting supper when I went over tonight, but there was just Karen, resting on the sofa. I went right to the stove and pulled over a frying pan. When I asked if I could get her something, she said just a cup of hot water.

I had trouble meeting her eyes when I took the cup over to her. That hurt-kid feeling was taking over. She took hold of my wrist and twisted it until I looked at her.

I almost smiled. Mostly, though, I wanted to cry.

She said she was sorry for the way she'd spoken to me the other day. She said it had had nothing to do with me and everything to do with her own disappointment over the baby.

I wanted to say something. I wanted badly for everything to be right between us. But something held me back.

"I'm not your only concern," I finally managed to tell her.

She said yes, I wasn't her only concern. I wasn't even one of her big ones anymore. But I would always be one of her treasured ones.

I had to look away then. A part of me wanted to rest my head against her shoulder and be soothed. But another part of me refused to be a motherless boy any longer. Even if she hadn't apologized, I would have to have gotten over it.

Suddenly I knew what I was struggling with. It wasn't just her feelings about me or the need not to take everything to heart. It was the fact people couldn't always give me all I was looking for.

It seemed the important thing was to take what they could give—the good, not the bad, and let it go at that. What one could not give me, maybe someone else could. Maybe I'd even find some things in myself. As for the bad—much of it had nothing to do with me anyway and needed to be left behind. Like the time with Karen.

I looked at her truthfully, then squeezed her arm and went back to getting supper.

MARCH 29, 1911

The going up to Lockridges' was hard today, with drifts blown across the road. Sue-Babe's extra load, a lamb on either side of the saddle in a gunny sack, didn't help any.

At the cemetery the fence was leaning under the weight of a snowbank. I thought how I wanted to be with John if there was another grave to be dug soon. I thought of my brother, too.

Someday we'd talk—Doug and I—though maybe we'd feel better not looking back. I don't know. I miss him more than I ever have before.

I was also thinking about Joe Lockridge. He built the cabin for Anna when he was nineteen and she sixteen. Sixteen. Only three years older than Joanna.

In three years, I will be almost twenty-one. That'll be

old enough to file, if I want to. It'll be older than Doug was when he got married.

Three years. Time enough to try out other things. College. Working on another ranch. Enough time to be sure of what I want. When I reached the gate at Lockridges', I'd planned my first move.

Shep set up a bark when he saw me on the hill. Joanna was pouring grain into a trough for a crowd of noisy sheep. She swung around to see who was coming.

"Sandy! It's been so long," she said when we met at the bottom. And she ran to tell Aunt Bea I'd come. It was like being home.

I carried the lambs to the barn and Joanna followed with Sue-Babe, leading her into a stall and pulling off the saddle as though there were no doubt at all I would be staying awhile.

We watched one of the lambs bound across the pen like it couldn't wait to try things out in a new place. The other one—Orphan—was different. He quivered against the railing, not knowing where he was or what was expected of him. I sat back in the straw and pulled him onto my lap.

Joanna knelt beside me and stroked him on the shoulder. I told her about Karen. She listened somberly and said it'd been real hard on Karen last time.

"That's all right, boy. That's all right," she said to Orphan. I told her I wouldn't have minded keeping him myself. She said I must have him then, that John wouldn't mind.

I told her maybe not, but for now Orphan was going to stay with the best shepherd in Western Wyoming. She grinned and gave him a nudge of encouragement.

I drew up my legs and rested my chin on my knees. I didn't know how to tell her what I'd been thinking the last stretch of the ride up. It would not be easy for her. I felt as though Karen were standing in the corner frowning at me.

I frowned to myself. But it occurred to me that at least I was different from my father. In my situation he'd have no thought at all for the future. He'd continue to let things fall as they may without regard for anyone's welfare, including his own.

Joanna looked at me, puzzled.

"Have you ever wanted to go someplace?" I asked her. "To get on a train and go to the city?" She said sure she had. And someday she was going to. To Denver—when Karen went back for a visit. But first they'd have to arrange things for Aunt Bea.

I was surprised. Not just a little. She said she was going to ride on a trolley and see a moving picture. Maybe she'd even ride a bicycle.

"A bicycle?" I said.

"Yes! Have you ever ridden one?"

"No," I confessed.

"Maybe you should come to Denver with us!"

That's when I looked at the toes of my boots and told her I'd already be there. I could not meet her eyes. I felt I was deserting her.

She sat back in the straw. I told her I'd be leaving in the fall to go to college for a year. I asked if she'd ever thought of going to school herself. She said sometimes, but mostly she just liked to read.

Then I asked if she'd ever thought of living in the city. She smiled, amused, and said why would she want to do that? I had to smile, too. Why *would* she want to do that?

I took her hands in mine. And she did not pull them away like she had that other time. I thought of the dance and the sheepherder with his arm around her shoulders. I didn't want him doing that when I was gone. I wanted to make her promise not to marry that sheepherder.

She looked down at our hands. "Will you be back?" she said.

I wanted to promise her I would. I wanted to *know* I would be back. But I did not know, and I could not promise.

She raised her eyes. I swallowed. I saw in them the same hurt I felt and a resolve I'd seen before in the barn after the dance. I told her it was too soon to know what would come of things. . . .

I feel drained from all that's happened this week. I could sleep for days.

APRIL 2, 1911

John asked after supper if I've any interest in cattle. He slapped his forehead when I told him sheep have a certain appeal.

Since we were touching on the subject of the future, I said I'd be heading back to Denver in the fall after I help him drive the last of the sheep to Rock Springs.

He fell silent. I took it as a tribute. Finally, he said I'd know soon enough when I'm back in the city if ranch life is for me.

Karen was pleased. She said I won't regret taking a

year at the university no matter what I decide to do afterwards—that she herself found it good preparation for ranch life.

Later, John told me I could always find a place at the table here and a bunk near the Captain. I touched the brim of my hat in acknowledgment.

APRIL 10, 1911

I am learning to bake bread. The first loaves I carried outside and smashed with my hammer for the chickens. Karen says I'll get better.

She says the same thing about John, who used too much soap in the wash and left puddles of slippery water on the floor—one of which I slid in, losing a whole armload of wood across the kitchen.

Karen says if ranching fails, we could always get jobs on the stage. John says he'll put her in the bedroom if she has any more comments.

I like the three of us working together—Karen doing the bossing from the sofa. There seems to be more laughter. If she can keep from having the baby for another four weeks, there's a good chance it can survive.

John is being very strict with her.

APRIL 19, 1911

I've begun straightening up the bunkhouse. Am expecting Ed back week after next, and soon after that the other hands. I wonder if he's changed any. I'm going to ask him to show me how to carve wooden horse heads like the ones above the bed. Not that there'll be much time for that in summer.

I've been sorting through my things. There are pants that are too short—they'll go for patches, worn-out socks will go to rags. The coat that I came here in, I am saving for Joanna.

When I am back in Denver, I'd like to know that she is warm and that she thinks of me.

DATE DUE
